JON D. P

THE ADVENTURES OF
CAPTAIN PELS

Inquiries and Book Orders should be addressed to:

Great Writers Media
Email: info@greatwritersmedia.com
Phone: (302) 918-5570

ISBN: 978-1-957974-09-5 (sc)
ISBN: 978-1-957974-20-0 (ebk)

Rev 3/15/2022

(& Victoria, Nellie, Barbara, Paul, & Kenneth, too)

CHAPTER 1

"Victoria! Nellie! Are you awake?" Victoria had been half awake for over an hour because of a feeling that something was wrong.

"*I* am," said Victoria. She could hear the sound of the ocean waves crashing outside her window. The toy pirate ship that Capt. Pels had made her startled her at first because it sat right next to her bed, but the smell of the teak wood was comforting once she realized what it was.

"Wake your sister up because we are going on a mission," said Capt. Pels. The thick salt air stuck to Nellie's skin as she woke to the nudging of her sister, Victoria, who had just turned eight. Nellie was six, and together formed the crux of Capt. Pels defense for their island beach resort from the attack of pirates. The Pels family had been defending this island for years, albeit in a covert manner. To the outside world, the Pels family appeared to be an ordinary family. The truth became known to the girls when they reached their fourth birthdays and were barely old enough to understand good and evil. Victoria and Nellie usually spent the days playing and helping take care of their younger sister, Barbara, who was three years old. They began to understand that many of the bedtime stories their father would tell them were actually true.

The two youngest siblings in the family, Paul and Kenneth, ages two and ten months didn't understand the truth yet, but still unwittingly assisted in defending the small beach town from the seemingly constant onslaught of pirates. Paul had strength beyond that of many adults, even at age two. The fact that he threw great temper tantrums if his milk was not warmed to the exact desired temperature before being placed in his sippy cup limited his usefulness to the cause, however. Each Pels had some hidden talent, and it was classified as "superhuman" by the secret government agency that hired Great, Great Grandpa Pels. It was handed down through the bloodline, although no one knew what it would be, and it sometimes didn't show itself until age four or more.

CHAPTER 2

Pirates still exist in this day and age. They were in disguise when they came ashore. A family on vacation might be spies looking for vulnerable places to launch an attack on the island. As Nellie pulled her bathing suit on, she grabbed her sandals and headed downstairs to the kitchen. The Pels family lived in a small three-bedroom house and had to share one bathroom. It could be frustrating, but the proximity to the beach and the outdoor shower made it all worthwhile in the girls' eyes. Victoria was already eating an apple and drinking some Vitamin Water.

"Capt. Pels is already down at the beach hurry! up!"

"OK!" shouted Nellie.

"Lower your voice!" hushed Victoria, "You'll wake everyone up."

"Stop bossing me around." Nellie shot back.

"Both of you better start getting along. There is enough trouble out there for all of us. We don't need to be fighting within our family."

Nellie and Victoria looked up to see their mom (whom outsiders called Christine) standing at the door. Christine was usually out the door before anyone woke up. She swam a couple of miles in the ocean or ran or biked (or sometimes all three) along the beach.

"Your dad needs your help, and he is waiting for you."

The girls always liked referring to their dad as Capt. Pels when they were on a mission, even though at first it seemed silly.

"OK, we're leaving," the girls said in unison.

Nellie finished placing her watch around her wrist. It was no ordinary watch, and it had many gadgets. She had been training to use it over the last few months. By the time they got down to the beach, they could see where Capt. Pels had set up what appeared to be a large beach umbrella. The sun was rising, and there were a few people out walking along the beach. The girls sat down on a beach towel under the umbrella, set up about a half mile away from the shore center--away from any other families that might set up for the day--for a reason. After the girls sat down, they used Nellie's watch to scan the area for any lifeforms.

"No one within a mile," declared Nellie.

Victoria hit a button on the pole of the umbrella. A trap door opened quickly, and the girls found themselves beneath the beach in Capt. Pels' underground fortress.

The computer screens gave off a bright glow, and the girls could see, for the first time, that the big oil rigger that had been slowly moving from north to south across the horizon was a pirate ship in disguise.

"Good morning, ladies," said Dr. Callahan.

Victoria loved Dr. Callahan because of his thick Irish accent. She thought he always sounded polite even when he got angry if they misused one of his inventions—like the time the girls used one of his devices to shock some mean boys who were torturing a crab.

"True or false: Boys are better than girls in soccer." said Victoria to Dr. Callahan.

"My dear lady, that is one hundred percent false," he replied, bringing a huge grin to her face. "Let's get down to business, shall we? Your father is going to need all the help he can get. When you return topside to the beach, you will notice that there are now three large beach umbrellas all leaning into each other -- kind of like certain larger families might do when relatives join them at the beach. This will enable you to have a larger place at the top of the umbrella and serve as a lookout for you. I have used some of our latest technology which utilizes mirrors and projections to make you invisible to the human eye up there. Ah, yes! Here comes one of my assistants now." Through one of the cameras, the girls could see a man placing two more umbrellas just as Dr. Callahan had described.

"Now, let me get to the point of the surveillance. We learned that a team of pirates is coming ashore with the idea of poisoning all of the pizza sauce on the island," said Dr. Callahan.

"Why?" asked Victoria.

"Why do pirates ever do anything?" he replied.

"Ahh, money," chimed in Nellie.

"Correct…my dear!" continued Dr. Callahan. "The idea, we believe, is to not only have the poison but also the only known cure and hold the island hostage. I will need each of you to begin spying immediately. If there are no questions, let's get moving."

CHAPTER 3

Nellie walked down a short hallway to the section of the underground fortress that led up to the beach umbrellas. She peeked her head up and through a trap door under a beach towel without being noticed and climbed out. After being assured that, still, no one was around, Nellie climbed up the beach umbrella poles and made her way to the top. She was amazed at the gadgetry Dr. Callahan had stored up there. She walked around top of the three umbrellas and noticed the standard computers, infrared goggles, laser guns, and other weaponry. What surprised her was what appeared to be a kite. Nellie pushed a button on her watch.

"Why does there appear to be a kite up here Dr. Callahan?" asked Nellie.

"Because there is a kite up there, my dear," he said. "Let me explain," he continued. "The kite is not, of course, just a kite, but a manned surveillance tool."

"Manned?" asked Nellie.

"Well, perhaps I should more accurately state 'girled' in this case."

"What?" said Nellie.

"Look, this kite, if you look at it close enough, it has space for you to slide into so that you can blend in and become part of it. Don't worry about whether there is enough wind to get you off the ground because, it is equipped with a small and silent engine that will allow you to maneuver it within a few miles of the shore and soar fairly high up in the sky."

"You want me to go one mile up in this thing?" said Nellie.

"Don't worry, it is safe. I promise."

Just then, Nellie heard some noises down below. She peeked in through the computer monitor and noticed that her younger brother Paul was playing under the umbrella. "Camouflage," thought Nellie. It was customary to have the entire family playing in and around the umbrellas so as to not draw attention to them.

Meanwhile, Victoria was busy walking with her scuba gear in an underground tunnel that continued until she was actually under the ocean. Victoria's extraordinary superhuman skill was her ability to swim fast. She could hold her breath for a long time, but the scuba gear was a pleasant option for her this morning. Awaiting her was a small submarine on which she would ride to get to the ship. It was more of a propeller on a big teardrop shape which you just held onto as it moved. Her mission was simple: swim under the tanker undetected to place a surveillance device on the bottom of the ship and determine if some plot to poison the island's pizza sauce was underway. She felt a bit nervous but knew that once she got started, everything would be fine. "I wonder where Dad…I mean, Capt. Pels is?" she thought.

A few miles up from the island, on what is called The North Shores, Capt. Pels was busy digging a trench and setting up a trap where he believed the most violent pirates would be coming ashore. He needed to dig deep enough to be able to hide and fit in some equipment. There he would wait. A few hundred yards behind him, what seemed to be a parrot stood watching his every move. Capt. Pels did not know it, but he had walked right smack dab into a trap.

CHAPTER 4

Nellie felt the strap tighten around her waist as she pulled it and clicked it. "Barbara, can you hear me?" asked Nellie. "Yeath, I am here," Barbara replied. Barbara was only three years old and had a lisp. Occasionally it would seem not so tiny and not so little.

She was capable (as is often the case) of doing more things at an earlier stage than her sisters, simply because she had the benefit of having her sisters from whom to learn. "Well, let's rock and roll," stated Nellie. Barbara's tiny but strong legs began running as fast as they could move away from the umbrella, while holding a kite string in her right hand. After about fifty yards, she felt the line become taught. Nellie then hit "go" on her remote control, and the kite gently and silently began to lift off the top of the umbrella. The system still needed a person to pull it, although this was more for cover so no one would notice that a kite was flying by itself. Barbara was just old enough to appear as if she was capable of flying this kite. The breeze and sounds of the ocean waves below Nellie made her thankful to be where she was, and there was no happier feeling than starting to fly higher and higher into the morning sky.

Nellie looked to her right, and a seagull was floating on the wind right next to her. "This is what it feels like to fly," she thought. Everything seemed to be perfect. Once she was up to 400 feet, she could use her instruments to peer in on the oil rig/pirate ship. "Everything is perfect," she thought, but...unbeknownst to Nellie, the string of the kite had become entangled on a large rock, and with the speed at which Nellie was climbing would cause her kite to jettison towards the earth.

Meanwhile, back at the tunnel, Victoria was just about nearing its end. It was about a half mile long, and she figured she must be pretty deep under the ocean at this point. Victoria reached the end, looked up and saw a rusty hatch with a ladder leading up to it. She was instructed to climb the ladder, put on her scuba gear, and climb through the other side. She then resealed and screwed the hatch back into place. She pulled a heavy lever, and slowly the great ocean from above began to pour into the hatch where she was sitting. Within seconds the water was up over her head. She checked her regulator. "Everything is ok," she thought. She slowly inflated her vest and floated out into the big, bright, clear blue waters. Her depth gauge showed that she was thirty feet below the surface. "Perfect," she thought. She looked to her right and left and grabbed her portable submarine. Nothing seemed amiss. She began swimming away from the hatch and towards the pirate ship, and felt something brush up against her back. With all the surveillance Dr. Callahan had done over the year, it never occurred to him that the pirates would have been able to accomplish mechanical sharks, capable of swimming at faster speeds, and programmed to eat anything that swam within a mile of the ship. Victoria had just crossed into the one-mile mark.

CHAPTER 5

Capt. Pels finished his digging and sat down. Christine had packed him a tofu sandwich with non-fat cheese and organic lettuce. While the flavor was not too great, the sandwich had all the qualities Christine wanted in a sandwich, which meant it contained zero grams of fat. Capt. Pels cursed to himself while biting into what tasted like bark and then thought, I will have to buy a slice of pizza later, assuming it is safe to eat. As he was thinking this, a flying parrot opened its beak and out flew a poisoned dart which hit Capt. Pels in his neck. He fell over, fast asleep. Within seconds, three pirates came up out of what looked like bushes and surrounded him.

The kite floated effortlessly until there was a sudden jerk. Nellie felt the string tug her down towards the earth.

"Barbara! What is going on?" Nellie screamed into her watch.

"This thing caught on a rock, and I cannot get it untied. Do something because the kite will crash." Then she turned the thrusters on her kite to full power and began to send the kite back up into the sky. The kite leveled out but could go nowhere because the line was tangled, and the pressure was putting awful stress on the engine. It was beginning to make funny sounds.

"I can't budge it," said Barbara.

"I'm doomed," said Nellie.

Barbara looked down, and noticed Paul sitting under the umbrella harmlessly for once in his life and playing with his trucks.

"I have an idea," she told Nellie. Barbara ran over to Paul and said, "Want some ice cream, Paul?"

"Ice cream! I want ice cream! Paul wants ice cream!" Paul threw down his trucks and looked at Barbara.

"Well, there ith ice cream under *thothe rockths* over there." She knew it was wrong to lie, but this was the only thing she knew that would motivate a two-year-old boy to drop his trucks and run to the rocks, which is exactly what he did.

"Ice cream!!" you could hear him yelling for miles away as he got to the rocks. He bent over and tried to move the large rock. "Heavy" he said sadly.

"There ith chocolate *thauthe* under there, too," said Barbara.

"Chocolate!" Paul bent over and with all his strength moved a rock that a grown man might not move.

"He is going to be really angry when he finds out," said Nellie, "but that is better than me crashing." Once the rock was lifted, the string came loose, and the kite gently righted itself and floated.

"NO ICE CREAM!! MOMMY! NO ICE CREAM," Paul was screaming and began stamping his feet on the beach so loudly that people started looking over at them even from a mile away.

"Paul, "*thettle*" down," said Barbara as she tried to think of ways to make him happy.

CHAPTER 6

The first time Victoria became aware that something was wrong was when she felt something swim past her and graze her scuba tank. She quickly turned around, and a large great white shark was swimming towards her. It was a robot great white shark with a video camera inside of its eyes. The pirates back in the ship saw Victoria's every movement. The shark started coming faster and faster towards her, and she seemed paralyzed with fear. The head pirate aimed the large razor-sharp teeth of the shark at the middle of Victoria. This will be fun and easy, sneered the other pirate who watched the live video feed in the main control cabin. The Great White Shark was less than ten feet away, but Victoria did not even try to escape. A group of pirates gathered around the screen to watch the carnage. A shock came over all of their faces. The diver swam away at the speed of what seems to be like a dolphin.

"Make it go faster!" the head pirate shouted.

"Arrrrr! I can't yee mate!"

"They are getting away," said another. To their surprise, Victoria stopped and turned, and then started swimming right for the shark.

"Victoria! this is Dr. Callahan. We have been watching you on the surveillance. It is not a real shark but a robotic one controlled by the pirates. You need to climb onto its back and cover its eyes with the black dye that we put in your watch. It will disrupt their surveillance, and they will not be able to see where you are going. That way, it will swim without seeing you until it runs out of power."

Victoria, in a winded and huffed tone said: "OK Dr. Callahan! Will do."

"ARRRRR, what are they doing?" asked a pirate.

Before anyone could answer, Victoria flew through the water and onto the back of the shark, blinding the camera.

"DUHHHH BOSSS, I THINK THEY ARE TRYING TO PUT SOMETHING ON THE CAMERA SO WE CAN'T SEE," said Brutus. Brutus was an overgrown pirate who stood nearly seven feet tall and weighed 400 pounds.

"ARRR, no kidding Brutus, how did you come up with that brilliant assessment?" barked Red Beard, the head of all the pirates.

"DUHHH, I JUST NOTICED THAT THE CAMERA IS NOW COVERED AND...."

"Shut up you fool, I was being facetious," said Red Beard.

Brutus turned to his fellow pirate friend Barney and said "DUH WHAT'S FACE E, FACE E, FACE E..."

"It means he was kidding, Brutus, and that he already knows they covered the camera with something."

"Oh!"

Victoria watched as the shark swam off into the deep dark ocean and then looked at her compass and began swimming towards the ship as her "submarine" had been damaged and no longer worked.

Capt. Pels awoke in the hull of a pirate ship handcuffed to the wall. Looking back, he was able to piece together very little of how he got there. His radio watch was damaged, and probably might not work. How could he notify his girls now of his situation?

CHAPTER 7

Nellie had been floating nearly a mile up in the sky and a mile out over the ocean. To the average person on the beach or boat, it appeared that there was just a kite flying, and she was able to gain infrared photographs of the "oil rig" and confirmed it was a pirate ship. What concerned her more was that she had seen men in a boat carrying what looked like an unconscious person onto the pirate ship. She could see through certain walls with her camera, but she still could not identify the unconscious person. From her vantage point, she could see down through the clear ocean water below, and before making radio contact, she was able to see her sister Victoria approaching the pirate ship.

"Victoria, I am floating a few hundred feet over you. How is it going?"

"Other than fighting off a shark, pretty well." Victoria replied.

"I saw some pirates carry an unconscious person onto the ship. I'm getting a little bit concerned. I've been trying to check in with Dad, I mean Capt. Pels, and he is not responding. Dr. Callahan has sent Barbara to see if she can find him."

"I haven't been able to reach him either. I am worried also," replied Victoria.

"Ladies, this is Dr. Callahan. Can you hear me?"

"Yes," each replied.

"Your dad is nowhere to be found. Barbara is on her way back to the umbrellas. I fear that the pirates may have something to do with this. Victoria, I need you to see if you can find out anything about this without being caught."

"Will do," said Victoria.

"Be careful," said Nellie.

Victoria swam directly underneath the ship and was able to latch onto the bottom without being detected. She, like Nellie, had equipment that would allow her to see life forms within the ship. Victoria attached a device to the bottom of the pirate ship and ran some scans of the interior. She was able to learn that there were 403 pirates on board. This is going to be difficult. There was also one person being held captive in a room near the starboard side of the ship. If she honed the camera in on this form, she could determine at a minimum if it was Capt. Pels.

"Dr. Callahan, they've caught Dad," was what Nellie and Barbara overhead Victoria say.

"We've got to rescue him," replied Nellie.

As Victoria was about to detach herself from the bottom of the massive ship, she saw something that amazed her. A few hundred feet below the pirate ship, the ocean floor opened up, and out came a giant whale and in each of the eyes was a pirate.

It was yet another mechanical sea creature. The pirates had also managed to create an underground fortress of their own and one that was very sophisticated.

Victoria remained perfectly still while the robotic whale swam by, and then she reported back to Dr. Callahan and the girls. They created a plan to both rescue Capt. Pels and find out more about the underground fortress. Victoria had enough oxygen in Dr. Callahan's specially designed tank to swim to the bottom and stay for several hours.

That evening, Nellie and Barbara approached the ocean. They quickly and quietly placed a mini submarine in the water and got in. The sub carried them under the water to the spot where Victoria had been hiding. Victoria had been monitoring and could detect no movement from the underwater door to the pirate's fortress. As the sub approached, Victoria saw a package Jettison from the back of it. Victoria swam to it and deployed an underground tent. She set it up near some rocks and coral and placed seaweed over and around it, so, that it was not noticeable. Dr. Callahan had designed a special sealant around it that would make it undetectable to radar, sonar, or the very infrared-based cameras the girls themselves used. The submarine was stashed behind it, and all three girls came inside. After setting up the sleeping bags for the night, the girls had a quick dinner and got a special message from Dr. Callaha regarding the security that the pirates might employ when the girls attempted to break into the underground fortress. They all decided to get some sleep, as they knew the task before them was monumental.

Paul was busy pounding on a toy truck of his such that it was nearly flat and under the sand. He walked over to his grandfather to see what he was saying.

"Paul, come here, you won't believe this," said Papa. Paul was looking at Papa as he explained what Kenneth was doing. Papa yawned and stretched and then took off his glasses and continued to talk to Paul. The problem was that Paul had scurried away to play with his toy, and Papa's vision was not good without his glasses. A seagull had flown onto the blanket and stood just about where Paul had stood. "What do you think of Kenneth? Pretty amazing, isn't it? Should we call your mom and tell her?" said Papa.

The blurry thing that was standing where Paul had stood replied, "CAWL, CAWL."

"OK Paul, you don't have to scream," said Papa. I'll call her now.

"CAWL, CAWL," said the seagull again.

"OK, Paul, I can hear you. You do not need to scream."

Dr. Callahan, who had been watching the whole thing on closed circuit TV, laughed out loud. The site of Papa having a conversation with a seagull offered a break from the tense situation. "The girls will get a kick out of this. Now we need to get them home safely," he thought.

CHAPTER 8

Capt. Pels sat staring at the wooden bench in his cell on the pirate ship. For all the technology that the pirates employed these days, they had used primitive handcuffs. After the changing of the last guard, Capt. Pels pushed out a universal key that could adapt to many locks. Every time he went on a mission, he hid the key on the underside of his tongue. He was able to maneuver the key so that it entered the lock and unlocked the cuffs. Within minutes, the cuffs were off. Capt. Pels tip-toed to the door and saw a pirate drinking a bottle of rum and leaning back in an old wooden chair. Perfect! thought Capt. Pels.

Victoria awoke to the feeling of water drops hitting her forehead. She sat up quickly and in a slight panic. "What are these from?" she thought. After inspecting the camouflaged tent roof, her fears were realized. The tent was leaking, some one hundred plus feet under the ocean. She could perhaps make it to the top, but she was worried about her younger sisters. The plan had been to wait it out in the tent and observe until an exact time to infiltrate the underground fortress could be found. After a quick thought, Victoria knew those plans had to be scrapped. She woke Nellie and Barbara.

"Victoria, I wath athleep," said Barbara with a furrowed brow.

"The tent is leaking. We have to infiltrate the fort now," shouted Victoria. The girls hustled and put on their scuba gear. As they made it to the hatch, the water leak began to get larger and larger. The water began to pour into the underground tent. Victoria helped Barbara, then Nellie out of the hatch, and as she was ready to escape, her scuba tank fell off. She reached for it as the water poured down on her, pinning her to the floor. The other girls watched in horror as Victoria used all her might to reach her tank. With every last ounce of energy she had, she was able to connect the tank to the regulator, all the while holding her breath and finally escaping.

Nellie and Barbara helped her over to the seaweed, where the girls hid. Victoria was ok, but she would not be much help the rest of the way. No sooner had the girls caught their breath when the ground above the fortress began to slowly open. A huge humpback whale meandered out through the large opening, and the girls could see pirates peering through the large eyes of the whale.

"We have to go now!" said Nellie.

All three girls swam as hard as they could and made it through the hole just as it was closing. They heard a large clanking sound as the two halves of the hole reconnected. The water began to drain, and the girls started floating towards the bottom. They managed to get to a pirate sub on the bottom and hide behind it. After all the water had drained the girls noticed that there were all kinds of mechanical submarines in the form of whales, sharks, and even large squids. They removed their scuba gear and hid by the door. Nellie was able to use a hairpin and unlock the door. That was easy enough, they all thought.

Inside was a long hallway, and at the end, there was a large steel vault-like door that would not be so easy.

"There is no way I can pick that lock," said Nellie.

Victoria noticed that ten feet above the door was a small air vent.

"OH, Barbara," said Victoria. Barbara was blessed with a miraculous talent, being able to leap like a fleet-footed ballerina, only much higher than most ballerinas older than she.

"That looks kind of high," said Barbara.

"You gotta try," said Nellie. Barbara ran to the end of the hall and began a sprint to the vault door, where Victoria and Nellie stood arms together, ready to thrust Barbara into the air. As Barbara landed on the girls' arms, they both thrust upwardly, and Barbara did a flip and landed perfectly onto the vent where she was hanging on for dear life.

"You can do it," whispered Nellie. Barbara was able to pry open the vent grate with one hand and crawl through the opening. After a few seconds, the door was unlocked, and Nellie and Victoria opened the door to a smiling Barbara who performed a perfect pirouette as a grand finale.

CHAPTER 9

Capt. Pels waited for the pirate drinking his rum to doze off as he knew he would. He managed to handcuff him in his cell and switch clothes with him and then lock the door. Capt. Pels was now in perfect disguise. In no time, Capt. Pels had made it to Red Beard's quarters and went to work trying to learn as much as possible about why these pirates were here in such large numbers, how they had developed this technology and how to defeat them.

Capt. Pels had found several documents that showed that poisoning the pizza sauce was just the beginning of the pirates' plans. The ultimate goal was to overrun the quiet and peaceful beach town and turn it into the pirates' island. No more churches, no more laws, no more children or families. Just chaos.

A large room as big as a warehouse with a large computer system at the very end awaited the girls at the end of another long hallway. A pirate stood guard over the computers and marched around them in a circle as much as a pirate could march.

"Nellie, we'll need your speed to get under the table on which the computers sit," said Victoria.

Every thirty seconds, the pirate would turn his back on where the girls were and start marching away from them, which allowed Nellie to sprint fleet-footed to the table and slide underneath just as the pirate turned around.

Nellie's heart pounded as she tried to catch her breath and be as quiet as possible. She could hear the boots of the pirate click as he marched past. She waited until the pirate started walking away again and then quickly logged onto the computer. She was able to run a couple of quick computer formulas that allowed her to find out the password for the entire pirate computer network. When she saw what the password was, she began to giggle. Nellie controlled her laughter and wrote down the password: pink tutu. "Pink tutu, what an odd password for a pirate," she thought. She waited again until the pirate turned and then sprinted back to Victoria and Barbara.

The girls quickly stepped out of the room, going down to the hallway where the mechanical whales and sharks were located. They hid behind a shark and waited and hoped and prayed that the hole would open soon so that they could help Capt. Pels. Victoria called Dr. Callahan with the good news, and he immediately began trying to infiltrate the pirates' computer system. Nellie looked up just as a loud hissing sound began. The room started to fill with water.

"Get your gear on," said Nellie, "we're about to escape." The room filled quickly, and the girls gently floated to the top. As the hole in the ocean floor opened up, a large mechanical whale began to swim in, and the girls were able to swim out behind it undetected, or so they thought.

"We need some help," said Victoria.

She began to make a loud clicking noise - caaa caaa caaa ti ti ti ti ti ti and off in the distance, a school of dolphins got the message: Capt. Pels' girls needed help. The dolphins began swimming for the girls.

"It's Marmalade," said Nellie referring to the mom dolphin who was leading the school to the girls. Marmalade had a big smile on her face as she greeted the girls. Each girl grabbed onto the back of a dolphin and Victoria told them to start swimming towards the great pirate ship.

CHAPTER 10

Capt. Pels had scanned the documents that revealed all of the secret plans of the pirates. It was quite a large amount of information, and he was not sure if it would be able to transmit to Dr. Callahan via satellite. He was also concerned that the transmission might attract the attention of the ship's computer system. Scanning and downloading the information into a computer chip would have to do for now. At the back of the room was a large window, and it was a three-story drop to the ocean. While Capt. Pels did not have Victoria's extraordinary God-given swimming ability, the best plan would be to jump and begin a long swim to the beach. With any luck, he might be able to track down some dolphins or the girls and get the information to Dr. Callahan. Capt. Pels was certain that they were all searching for him at this very moment, and all he could think about was letting them know he was ok. He placed a tiny transmitter in Red Beard's cabin under a rug. Dr. Callahan had invented it, and it would allow for a remote detonation capable of sinking the ship once they gave a fair warning for the pirates to vacate.

Capt. Pels walked to the window and looked down. "Here goes nothing," he said as he jumped out the window. His heart jumped a beat when he saw the sun beating on the top of the water so far below. He seemed to suspend in mid-air for a moment. His thoughts raced to all that had happened to him in life, and he thought about his three brave girls and hoped they were ok. He looked toward the beach island off in the distance several miles and wondered how everyone was doing back at the umbrella camp. Then, suddenly, the breeze from falling rushed upon him as he quickly began falling towards the water. About one mile from the pirate ship and a few hundred feet under the ocean, a school of dolphins, with the girls in tow, sped towards the ship. The girls felt the ocean water rush by them as the dolphins moved swiftly through the water. Off in the distance, Barbara could see the outline of the great ship and started to get a little nervous and a little excited. She thought about rescuing her dad, and this kept her motivated.

Capt. Pels' feet hit with a great crash as he reached the ocean, and then suddenly, all was quiet as he slipped deeper into the water and dropped to a depth of thirty feet. He knew he could hold his breath for a few minutes, and he thought this would be best in case the splash or noise had caught the attention of anyone on the ship. Feeling disoriented from the plunge, Capt. Pels' relied on his previous training and blew a bubble out of his mouth, then followed it as it rose to the surface. Many people had drowned by actually swimming deeper into the water, thinking they were swimming to the surface. Following the bubbles was a not so obvious method in times of panic. Still, the bubble had a long way to go to get to the top. "I hope the girls are ok," was the last thing he remembered thinking.

Dolphins have amazing underwater senses, and a large splash in the distance caught the attention of Marmalade. After a few quick turns she had an object clearly in sight and started swimming to it. Barbara shouted through her gear,

"Hey... look!" as they saw Capt. Pels swim towards the ocean surface.

"We've found Capt. Pels and can go back to the beach," thought Victoria as the dolphins approached him. By the time they reached him, he was exhausted and out of breath.

"Grab a hold," said Nellie and Capt. Pels reached his arms out and embraced one of the dolphins. The girls gave him a regulator, and he put it in his mouth so he could breathe underwater. Instantly, he started to feel better.

"Let's head back to the beach," urged Victoria, but before they could begin, she felt something moving behind her.

CHAPTER 11

As Barbara turned around, she noticed the wide jaws of a mechanical shark staring her down. Within seconds, they were all surrounded by mechanical sharks and one whale.

"Surrender? Or we will attack yeeee...mate...," shouted a pirate from behind one of the whale's black huge eyes.

"Ahhh, yee mate, I'd surrender now," said another. Before anyone could do anything, Barbara was in the grasp of the jaws of the shark. Nellie pulled out a laser harpoon gun and aimed it at them.

"No! Do not hurt Barbara, and we will surrender," shouted Capt. Pels.

Capt. Pels and the girls were brought aboard to Red Beard. "Aye, did you think you would walk out of here so easily?" he said. "We have been watching yee all the time," he continued. "Take them to the prison chamber," shouted Red Beard.

"DUUH OK BOSS," said Barney, the overgrown pirate.

As they were walking away, Red Beard said, "Ahhh, yee feed them to the sharks instead. I want them to walk thee... plank."

"BUT DAHHH…BOSS, WHAT ABOUT THE LITTLE GIRLS?" said Barney.

"Feed them to the sharks, you fool!"

Barney hung his head low but did follow what the boss ordered. He started walking with several other pirates helping to escort Capt. Pels and the girls to the plank.

The other pirates jeered at Capt. Pels, "Ahh, yee this the end Capt. Pels, yeeeerrrr not so brave now, are you?" they snickered.

"Yeeeerrrr faith is lost now, I'd say," said a pirate with a large scar over his face. He jabbed Capt. Pels with a sharp knife.

At the other end of the ship, dozens of more pirates waited as Capt. Pels and the girls approached the long makeshift wooden plank. They jeered and shouted at them when they came. They threw trash at Capt. Pels and some jumped up and down in excitement at the anticipated carnage.

"Ahhh, yee see, crime does pay! Hee hee hee hee," whined one.

They pushed Capt. Pels out first, with a sharp sword towards the end of the plank. The hoots and howls of the pirates grew louder. Down below, Capt. Pels could see the sharks circling, and some given the mechanical control by the pirates, jumped out of the water and clamped their jaws together, making a loud smacking noise. This brought delight to the pirates. Barney looked down at little Barbara and saw a smiling face.

"I forgivth you," she said.

Something happened deep down in Barney's heart, and a large tear formed in his eye. "Do I enjoy this life?" he thought. The constant insults and backstabbing of people who were supposed to be his friends? He never liked that they stole and robbed and even hurt some people, but he had no other choice. This was the only place where people weren't afraid of his large size. As a boy, he tried to fit in, but never could. He never knew his father and mother, and without anyone who ever seemed to care, fell in with the wrong crowd. There was no reason for him to know right from wrong, yet seeing this little girl with blonde curly hair saying, "I forgivth you" made him rethink this life. Barney looked up to see the sword being stuck into the back of Capt. Pels as he was just inches from the end.

"NOOOOOOOOO," shouted Barney as Capt. Pels fell off the end of the plank.

CHAPTER 12

Capt. Pels had one last trick up his sleeve and used a ballet maneuver he had learned from little Barbara.

"You juth reach your armths high up in the air and grab the bar asth you fall by," he could still hear her saying this as he clasped the plank with his two arms, causing the plank to recoil and turn, flipping him back up and over the plank onto the ship where he landed with all the skill of Barbara.

"Awethome," shouted Barbara as Barney started pushing pirates around as if they were rag dolls. At nearly 400 pounds, it was easy to see that none of them were any match for him.

He picked up Barbara and the girls in one arm and started running - lumbering really - towards the other side of the ship. Capt. Pels struck hard and fast. Within seconds, five pirates were laying on the ground holding their heads, victims of Capt. Pels' precision left hook and uppercut punches. However, there were dozens more who saw the commotion and started chasing them.

Barney knew of an escape hatch at the other end of the ship. He was making his way to help the girls as fast as he could. Capt. Pels was fighting back the pirates to buy them more time. As he swung as fast and as hard as he could, he noticed a pirate who had a remote control in his hand for one of the sharks. Captain Pels jumped up and over a large wooden crate and dove onto this pirate, knocking the remote control loose. As he picked it up and ran towards the escape hatch, he looked back to now see hundreds of pirates on deck running towards them.

Barney kicked open the trap door to the hatch, and Nellie shouted, "Cooooooooool." Inside the door was a long slide which ran the entire length of the oil tanker and ended in the ocean.

"DUUUHH WE CAN SLIDE TO THE OCEAN HERE, BUT THOSE SHARKS WILL BE OVER TO THIS SIDE OF THE SHIP IN NOOOO TIME," said Barney.

"Don't worry about those sharks, guys," shouted Capt. Pels. "Victoria, give me your watch," Victoria took off her watch and threw it to Capt. Pels. Capt. Pels got onto the long sliding board first, making sure the girls were right behind him. "Let me go first to deal with the sharks."

Behind him and the girls, Barney followed. Barbara looked back at Barney, who was confident and sure of himself on the ship, and saw how nervous he looked.

"What's wrong Barney?" she shouted as they all began to slide at a rapid speed down the slide.

"I CAN'T SWIM," he shouted back.

"Don'th worry, we are all greath sthwimmerths, and my dad, I mean Capth Pels, will help and get the dolpihnths I'm thure," Barbara reassured.

Meanwhile, Capt. Pels was busy entering data into Victoria's watch. "Dr. Callahan, can you hear me?" he said.

"My good Captain, is that you?" replied Dr. Callahan, punctual as usual.

"It is indeed. I hope you are at your computer station because we've got about thirty seconds until we reach the end of this slide, and I am going to e-mail via satellite some information which should allow you to send a virus to the pirates' network," said Pels.

"Outstanding!" replied Callahan, "I have the password from the girls' recon mission but needed one last bit of information, which, if you are sending what I think you are sending, should do it."

Capt. Pels hit 'send' as soon as he downloaded information from the remote control, grabbed it from one of the pirates as he, Barney, and the girls reached the middle of the slide. Off in the distance, at the end of the slide, Capt. Pels saw a terrible site. The sharks had already been deployed to this side of the ship and in fact, were waiting for them with mouths agape.

CHAPTER 13

Nellie could not believe that there existed a slide this long in an oil rig/pirate ship. Although they were sliding so fast, it seemed like slow motion being the slide was so long. She could see Victoria in front of her and Capt. Pels beyond that. Barbara and Barney followed her. Together they were all heading towards the end of the slide and towards the water. She closed her eyes briefly and said a prayer. Up behind her at the top of the slide, she could hear the pirates. She looked back and had a hard time seeing around Barney but could see enough to notice that the pirates were following them, swords in hand, down the slide.

Capt. Pels called out to Dr. Callahan, "Hurry, good doc, we're running to the end of the road, er, slide."

"I'm sending the message now," said Dr. Callahan.

Dr. Callahan sent an electronic e-mail via satellite with the appropriate password to the mainframe computer system for the pirates' network. The signal went out into space from the beach umbrellas, bounced off a satellite, and was rerouted to the pirate ship and underground fortress a few hundred feet beneath the ocean by an ultrapulsed signal he had developed. The e-mail virus was sent to the pirates' mainframe computers, and within a split second, the mainframe computers sent a signal to all of the mechanical sharks and whales and created a major malfunction in them.

Each closed its mouth and fell harmlessly to the ocean floor. The next command sent a signal to the fortress and the ship to self-destruct in five minutes.

"Dr. Callahan, I need you to patch me through to every pirate on that ship, including Red Beard," said Capt. Pels. He delivered the following message: "Attention all pirates on deck or below in the underground hidden (at least previously hidden) fortress: this is Capt. Pels, I have sent a computer virus to your mainframe commanding that the ship and fortress self-destruct in five minutes. You have been warned to vacate immediately or face the consequences."

Capt. Pels and the girls, along with the oversized Barney, plopped into the ocean with smiles on their faces. Victoria quickly swam below and freed the dolphins so that Barney (who could not swim) could stop grabbing onto everyone to stay afloat. The dolphins took everyone briskly away, and the remaining pirates finally made it to the end of the sliding board. Nellie looked back to them swimming towards the horizon and grabbing onto lifeboats.

She even could hear Red Beard screaming, "AHHH YE EEE MAAATEEES, LE T 'S E RRRRR G E T OUTTA HERE!"

CHAPTER 14

The rush of the ocean breeze flowing through her hair on the back of the dolphin made Barbara giggle. In the distance, she could see everyone back on the beach by the three umbrellas.

Grandma was waiting when they returned by the water's edge, and she could hear the sound of steel drums coming from the radio of her mom, who was sitting with Kenneth and Paul, each of whom had on a big smile.

"Let's get some ice cream to celebrate," said Grandma. The girls could think of nothing better to do on a warm summer night on a beach island.

Dr. Callahan put on his colorful floral button-down shirt and beach hat to join them. The dolphins dropped everyone off at the beach and the girls noticed in the distance the ship heading towards the horizon.

"Capt. Pels, the ship is escaping," said Victoria.

"Don't worry, I fibbed a little about the five-minute detonation, and programmed the ship to go out to sea for a few miles where it will sink without notice and never be heard from again."

Christine took Capt. Pels' hand and Nellie and Barbara scooped up Kenneth. Dr. Callahan and Grandma, and Grandpa with sun-tanned skin, walked towards the boardwalk a mile or more away so that everyone could get a large scoop on a waffle cone.

"I love my life," thought Victoria as she followed everyone. Tomorrow, she'd swim in the ocean and ride some waves. "My friends will never believe me," she thought, "Oh well."

THE END

CPSIA information can be obtained
at www.ICGtesting.com
Printed in the USA
LVHW070719190422
716592LV00021B/853

9 781957 974095